Secrets of the Forest

Colleen L. Reece

REVIEW AND HERALD® PUBLISHING ASSOCIATION
HAGERSTOWN, MD 21740

This book was
Edited by Faith Johnson Crumbly
Cover design by Cal Bausman
Cover and interior illustrations by Mary Bausman
Typeset 14/16 Century Schoolbook

01 00 99 98 97   5 4 3 2 1

PRINTED IN U.S.A.

R&H Cataloging Service
Reece, Colleen Loraine, 1935-
    Secrets of the forest.

    1. Natural history—Juvenile works.   I. Title.

                    508

ISBN 0-8280-1067-6

Dedication

Special thanks
to my brother Randy
and niece Julie
for serving as resource persons.

Note to Readers

I grew up a few miles outside of the little western Washington logging town of Darrington. Tall mountains and deep forests surrounded our home. Hundreds of times our family climbed over the fence, crossed the logged-off fields, and trooped down to Dan's Creek and the Sauk River. Our woodsman father and teacher mother opened a new world to my brothers and me with their endless supply of nature lore. We grew up with a love and appreciation for the many curious things in God's handiwork.

It costs nothing to see the wonders of creation. All we have to do is to follow Dad's advice in the story, "Learn to stop, look, and listen."

If you like mysteries, come along with Cari and Andy and discover with them the secrets of the forest.

Your author friend,
Colleen L. Reece

Contents

1

Builders

ive-year-old Cari Reynolds and her 10-year-old brother Andy sat on the top step of their home in western Washington. They stared at each other, then at Dad.

"You mean, no—no—trip this summer?" Andy stammered.

Cari felt as disappointed as Andy sounded. "No trip?" she echoed.

Dad's blue eyes smiled even before his mouth did. "That's the bad news. The good news is that God helped our doctor find out what will help Mom get well. She needs lots of rest and good food."

"Maybe she'll get better soon. Then we can still go on a trip," Andy suggested and smiled.

Cari's heart sank when Dad shook his head and said, "Not this summer. But there's more good news. The weather has been so hot my work in the woods has to be done very early in the morning. That means I'll get home a little after lunch. If you two can manage to tidy up the place and take care of fixing lunch, we can have a lot of fun together in my free time. OK?"

"All right!" Andy cheered. A big grin crept over his tanned face.

"We can do it," Cari said. "Mom showed me how to butter bread and make sandwiches."

"I'm a good cleaner," Andy put in. He wrinkled his forehead. "Hey, Dad, how can we have fun when Mom's sick?"

Dad smiled. "She needs to sleep in the afternoons. If we go outside, the house will be quiet."

"Where can we go?" Cari thought of trips they had taken to the beach, to big cities, and other exciting places.

Dad spoke softly. His eyes twinkled and grew big and round. "Do you know that not far from here there's a whole community with wonderful things to see and learn?"

"Come on, Dad, the only town within 30 miles is our little town, and we know all about Darrington," Andy said.

"Not Darrington. Besides, I said 'community,' not 'town.'"

"Same difference, isn't it?"

Cari burst out, "What com-com-community, Dad?"

"The forest!" Dad said. He laughed when the children looked surprised. "The forest is not just a bunch of trees and bushes. God put everything in the forest community we need to have a people community." He laughed again.

"Really?" Cari asked.

Dad nodded. "Yes, and all the plants and animals must do exactly what God created them to do. Each one is important."

"Are there teachers and doctors in the forest?" Cari asked.

Andy chuckled, but Dad said, "The forest has many secrets."

Cari could hardly wait for the next day.

Before they left home, Mom told them, "Your stay-at-home vacation is neat. It can go on all year long." When the children asked why, Mom wouldn't explain. She just said, "Wait and see."

"I don't see any teachers or doctors," Andy teased, running ahead down the trail.

"Hold it, son. You won't see anything until you learn to stop, look, and listen. Noise and movement always frighten wild animals." Dad put one finger to his lips.

Andy slowed down. Cari walked behind Dad, trying to step as quietly as he did.

"Every community needs builders," Dad said. He stopped walking and asked, "Do you see one?"

Cari and Andy looked and looked but had to give up. Then Dad pointed to a nest with a bird sitting in it.

"Oh!" Cari hurriedly covered her mouth with her hand. Andy admitted, "Yeah, that's a builder."

Soon they reached a stream blocked with fallen logs and branches. *Splash!* Something furry shot into the water.

"What's that!" Cari cried as she stared in the direction of the noise.

"I know!" Andy ran to the edge of the stream. "It's a beaver. That's its dam, and—hey! The beaver's a builder, too. Beavers cut down tree trunks with their teeth and build homes in the water."

"We must go now," Dad told the children.

"Too bad," Cari said. Then she waved and called, "Goodbye, beaver. Goodbye, little bird. We'll come again," and she ran after Dad and Andy. ●

2

Bankers

Hurry, Dad!" Cari called. "I'm ready to go."

"So am I." Andy bounced out of the Reynoldses' big, old white house and waited on the wide steps with his sister. "What forest secret will we see today?"

When Dad caught up with the children, Cari slipped her hand into his hand and skipped along beside him. Andy ran ahead to hold up the barbed wire on the fence so they could crawl underneath it.

"Today's secret of the forest can't be any better than the forest builders." Andy grinned. "I liked the beaver and its dam and the bird in the nest. Our stay-at-home vacation is almost as neat as going on a trip."

"I'm glad Mom's better." Cari crawled under the wire. "God's making her well. Right, Dad?"

"Right. And our doctor is helping Him. So is the extra rest Mom gets while we are outside exploring."

Cari looked at the trees and wildflowers. "I never, ever knew how much there was to know about the forest," she said.

"Me neither." Andy started to race down the trail but stopped and looked at Dad. "Sorry. You said we had to stop, look, and listen if we wanted to see things, didn't you?"

"That's right," Dad answered. "Movement and noise frighten forest animals. They hide so you can't see them."

After quickly walking across the field behind their house, the explorers went down the sloping hill where they sledded in winter. When they got to a woodsy place, Dad sat down on a big stump left by the loggers. He lifted Cari onto his lap and made room for Andy beside them. "Sit quietly," Dad said in a low voice. "Listen and see what happens."

At first all Cari could hear was her heart beating fast: *Thumpety thump! Thumpety thump!* Next she heard birds singing in the trees. At last a curious sound made her stretch her eyes wide open. "Brrscree. Brrscree." The noise came from a huge maple tree close by. What could be making that noise? Andy looked as puzzled as Cari.

The children sat stiller than still. So did Dad. The noise grew louder. Maple leaves rustled. Cari closed her lips tightly to keep from crying out. A branch of the maple tree swayed and bent. *Thud!* A gray squirrel with a bushy tail as big as its body landed on the ground not far from the stump where the Reynolds family sat.

Dad whispered so low that Cari and Andy had to lean close to him to hear what he said, "That fella is a forest banker."

A banker? The gray squirrel sat up on its hind legs, folded its front paws over its white chest, and peered at them. Cari struggled to keep from giggling. Andy put his hand over his mouth. The squirrel did look a little like Mr. Davis, the Darrington banker who always wore a gray suit and a white shirt!

Thud, thud, thud! Three more squirrels landed in the forest clearing that was circled with tall pine, fir, spruce, cottonwood, and willow trees. The squirrels played tag with one another. Next they busily hunted for cones and seeds.

Dad slowly took a handful of unshelled, unsalted peanuts from his pocket and dropped them on the ground. The squirrels scampered to the nuts, grabbed them, and ran back up the branches of the maple with their treasure. When all the peanuts had been taken, Cari wiggled. The squirrels immediately hid in the maple tree, but Cari could still hear "Brrscree. Brrscree."

"Let's see if we can find a bank," Dad said mysteriously. After searching for a few minutes, he called softly, "Come look." The children ran to him. Dad lifted Cari up so she could see into the hollow tree trunk.

"It looks like a bird's nest," she cried. "But there are shells and chewed-on cones in there."

"Let me see." Andy climbed up the tree and looked into the hole. "Wow!" he called down to Cari. "This place needs a good cleaning."

"In the fall this hollow tree will be stuffed with corn and nuts and other food. The squirrels put away food when it's available so they can eat in the wintertime," Dad said.

"Just like we save money for when we need it, huh, Dad?" Andy looked into the nest again, then slid to the ground.

On the way home, a tiny, striped chipmunk ran across the explorers' path. The tail pointed straight toward the sky. "Are chipmunks God's bankers, too?" Cari asked.

"Yes, but they live in tunnels in the ground instead of in trees."

"Builders and bankers. What will we find next?" Andy thought out loud.

Dad's blue eyes twinkled. "Wait and see!" ●

Supermarket

3

Supermarket

How good it was that Mom was able to be up for part of the day now. "I love being 5," Cari told Mom, who lay resting on the couch. "I love our stay-at-home vacation when Dad takes Andy n' me to learn forest secrets."

Cari counted on her fingers. "In God's forest com-com-mu-nity we saw a beaver and a bird in a nest. Dad said they're builders. We saw bankers, too. A chipmunk and some squirrels. They store stuff away." Cari giggled. "Mom, one of the squirrels kind of looked like Mr. Davis."

Mom laughed. Her blue eyes sparkled. "What will you see today?" she asked the children.

"I don't know." Cari jumped up. "I have to help Andy make lunch so when Dad gets home he can take us exploring again." Cari hurried to the big kitchen and helped 10-year-old Andy fix egg salad sandwiches with lots of lettuce. As soon as Dad came home, Andy poured big glasses of milk.

"Dad," Cari said during lunch, "when we need food, we go to the supermarket or get stuff from our garden. The forest doesn't have a supermarket, does it?"

Andy laughed and started to choke. Then he remembered how he'd laughed at the idea of forest builders and bankers. Maybe Dad knew some more forest secrets.

"The squirrels and chipmunks store up nuts, corn, and seeds," Mom reminded them.

"And the beavers eat tender bark and twigs and roots and water lilies," Andy chimed in.

"How do you know that?" Cari looked surprised.

Andy grinned. "I looked it up in our *World Book Encyclopedia* last night," he answered. "Beavers also store food for winter. They put logs and branches under the water near their lodges. In winter they swim under the ice and eat the bark."

"You're so smart!" Cari shouted.

It made Andy feel good to hear her say

that. "As soon as you learn to read better, you will get smarter, Cari."

Dad and Mom laughed. Mom said, "Don't forget that God created His animals to be pretty smart, too. They're wise enough to do what they need to do in order to live."

"God also prepared the forest to help out," Dad put in. A little later he showed them what he meant. On their walk he gave the children a little job. "See how many kinds of food you can spot."

"Salmonberries," Cari cried out. She popped a golden berry into her mouth.

"Wild strawberries. Yum!" Andy handed several berries to his sister and then filled his mouth.

"Huckleberries." Cari picked red and blue berries off bushes near her.

"We've already talked about nuts, seeds, and water lilies," Dad reminded the children. "Come to this part of the forest's supermarket." With one quick motion he turned over a rotting log. Fat white grubs clung to the wood.

"Yeccch. I pass!" Andy turned up his nose. So did Cari.

"Bears love grubs." Dad laughed. "I'm glad grubs aren't people food, though."

Next Dad showed them wild mushrooms. He warned them, "Never, never, *never* eat anything in the woods unless I tell you it is safe to eat. Mushrooms can be good, but some poisonous toadstools look a lot like mushrooms."

"We promise," the children said.

"What else is in the forest supermarket?" Cari asked.

"Lichens," Dad answered.

"Like ems?" Cari repeated.

"The word is *like-uns*," Andy said. "We studied about them in school. Insects and snails and slugs eat lichens."

"They can have them!" Cari said. She made a funny face.

"You'll like this better," Dad promised. He pulled a piece of pink clover blossom and then let Cari touch the blossom with her tongue.

"Why, it tastes like honey!" she exclaimed.

"You're tasting nectar," Dad explained. "That's why birds and bees love clover blossoms. Bees use nectar to make honey."

All the way home the family talked about the forest supermarket and how wonderful God is to make sure all His creatures have food. ●

4

Garbage Collectors

Andy quickly tied his tennis shoes and hurriedly put on a lightweight jacket. Even in summertime it could be cool under the trees in the woods.

"I wonder what we'll see today," Cari said as Andy raced out of the house. She sat on the wide back porch.

"I know one thing we *won't* see," Andy teased.

"What?" Cari demanded.

"A garbage truck like the one that goes around Darrington and picks up people's trash," Andy replied. He grinned. "There are no garbage collectors in the forest."

When Dad came outside with a backpack filled with sandwiches Cari had helped make, she jumped up and down. "I am so glad you have a whole day off and we can go see our forest com-community again," she said. "Will it be as neat as the forest supermarket we saw last time? The berry bushes and flowers with their nectar for bees, and . . ."

"I told Cari the one thing we won't see in the forest is a garbage truck," Andy said. "Right, Dad?"

Dad looked mysterious, the way he always did when he knew forest secrets the children hadn't learned. "Well . . ."

"We know. Wait and see," the children said together. Cari slipped her hand into Dad's. They called goodbye to Mom, who planned to take a nap, and quickly went to the barbed-wire fence at the edge of their property. They walked across the field, down the hill, and into the forest. Cari and Andy remembered to stop, look, and listen.

A little brown rabbit hopped by. When they stopped, it did too. It looked at them out of bulging eyes and twitched its nose. Cari stepped on a twig, and the frightened rabbit hopped into the bushes.

Just before they reached the Sauk River, a flash of yellow-gray whipped across the trail a little way ahead of them.

"Hey, Dad, what's a dog doing out here?

It doesn't look like any of the neighbors' dogs," Andy reported.

"That wasn't a dog. That was a coyote," Dad answered. "By the way, Andy, that coyote helps fill the job you talked about."

"You mean a garbage collector?" Andy's mouth fell open. Cari raised her eyebrows as she listened.

"In a way. God created the coyote to be one of the animals that keep the forest clean."

"How, Dad?" Cari tugged on his arm.

He patted her curly yellow hair. "You know that animals die when they get old or sick. They have no way to be buried. The forest would be a pretty sad place with dead animals all around, wouldn't it?"

Cari and Andy nodded.

"That's how coyotes serve as garbage collectors. They get rid of things that could make the woods unpleasant. Can you think of some other garbage collectors?"

"I know," Andy quickly answered. "Wolves. Except there aren't very many. Our teacher said people have killed too many wolves."

"That's right, and it's sad," Dad said. "People felt sorry for deer and other animals that the wolves killed. They sent hunters in to kill the wolves. They should never have done this. When there aren't enough wolves or coyotes to help keep the herds of deer free of the old and sick animals, the number of deer increases. There isn't enough food for them. Many starve."

"Then coyotes and wolves are good?" Cari asked.

"Everything God created is good in its own way," Dad said. "Sometimes people step in and try to change what we call the balance of nature. God adds and takes away things in nature to keep it balanced.

Andy scuffed the ground with his tennis shoe. "Then even that ugly old buzzard we saw last summer by the road is good for something? Hey! It's a garbage collector too."

"Yes," Dad agreed.

"Well, we didn't see a truck, but we *did* see a garbage collector." Cari laughed. "Wait till we tell Mom!" Dad hugged both children. ●

5

Doctors and Nurses

K now what would be fun, Cari?" Andy asked. "We could make a list of all the things in the forest community Dad has showed us. You can help by reminding me of some of the things we saw and talked about during our walks in the forest."

"Goody!" Cari clapped her hands. She loved helping her big brother but didn't often get the chance. "I still think the garbage collector, I mean the coyote, looked like a dog," Cari said.

"Yeah. It's sort of related," Andy agreed. "Not exactly a cousin, but sort of." Andy hunted up paper and marking pens. He wrote the words "Garbage Collectors" in bright-red letters at the top of one page.

Cari ran her fingers over each letter after it dried. She spelled, "G-A-R-B-A . . . I know what that is."

She watched Andy write "coyotes" in smaller letters beneath the heading, and she sounded out the word. "Coy-o-tes. What a funny way to spell it. I think it should be spelled K-Y-O-H-T-S." She giggled. "Don't forget to write 'wolves' and 'buzzards,' like Dad said."

"I won't," Andy promised.

Before Andy finished the list, Dad came home from work and it was time for lunch. He surprised them by saying, "We need the magnifying glass today."

"Why?" Andy wanted to know.

"Wait and see," Cari told him, just as Dad always did.

Andy rolled his eyes and laughed. Mom and Dad laughed too.

Mom made an announcement. "I'm feeling so much better that one of these days I can go to the forest. You can show me all the wonderful things God created that you've seen and learned about. I can hardly wait." Her cheeks turned pink because of her excitement.

"That's great!" The children hugged their mother, then followed Dad outside. Mom waved to them from the window.

"How would you like to see some doctors and nurses and a pharmacy?" Dad asked. When they reached the forest, he held up a branch for them to walk under.

"Sure," Andy agreed, but Cari wrinkled her forehead.

"What's a farm—whatever it is?" she asked.

"You know Mr. Adams at the store in town? He gives us the medicine the doctor prescribed for Mom. His store is a pharmacy."

"Farm-a-cy," Cari repeated the word. She liked the way the word rolled around on her tongue.

"Why did we bring the magnifying glass?" Andy asked.

"I want to show you what goes on in an anthill." Dad led them close to a nearby colony. The children looked at the swarming ants. "Don't get close enough to disturb them," Dad warned the children. "These ants bite. Just watch."

Cari looked at the ants. "Dad, they're fighting!"

"Yes, ants fight," Dad said. He pointed to reddish-looking ants fighting against black ants. "Just like people who can't get along. Use the glass, Cari."

At first Cari didn't like how huge the

ants looked through the magnifying glass. Then she got so interested in the anthill she forgot her fear. "Dad, some of the ants are hurt. Other ants are carrying them away!"

Andy squinted. "They sure are. Let me have the glass, Cari."

She handed it over.

He cried, "They really are taking the wounded away, just like doctors and nurses do in emergencies. All right!"

They watched the ants for a long time. Then Cari said, "I want to see a pharmacy where there's medicine."

"Me too." Andy handed the magnifying glass back to Dad.

"Sick animals chew grass," Dad told them. "See those flowers?" He pointed to tall stalks with purple and pink bell-shaped blossoms. "They're called foxgloves."

Cari reached out to the flowers, which looked like little mittens.

"Don't touch them, Cari!" Dad quickly told her. "The plant could poison you."

In his eagerness to see everything, Andy brushed against some pretty green plants. "Ow!" he howled and rubbed his arms where red bumps were swelling up. "That plant stung me."

"We'll use medicine from the forest pharmacy." Dad quickly crushed the broad leaves of a nearby plant and rubbed them on Andy's arm. "This plant is called 'dock' and grows by stinging plants called nettles," Dad explained.

"My arm feels better already," Andy said. "I'm glad God made dock as well as doctors!" ●

6

Exterminators

Every time Dad brought Andy and Cari back from a trip to the forest community, they told Mom all the things they had seen and learned. Andy also added the new things they learned to his growing list.

"I never knew the forest was so neat," Andy said. He carefully wrote the title "Doctors and Nurses, Pharmacy." Beneath the title he wrote these words: ants, grass, foxglove, dock.

Cari slapped at a mosquito that had slipped into the house when she accidentally left the screen door open. "Go away, pest! Don't bite me!" Cari yelled. The mosquito buzzed away from her, and Andy whacked it.

"Thanks, Andy." Cari pressed her nose against the windowpane and stared out at the gray, rainy world. "We won't get to go to the forest today. It's all wet and drippy."

"Yeah," Andy mumbled as he finished his work and laid down the marking pen. He looked disappointed.

Dad put down his newspaper. "Bundle up, kids. I'll show you some interesting things about nature right here in our garden." The twinkle in his eyes told Cari and Andy Dad had something fun for them to see. They put on their boots, raincoats, and hats, and followed Dad outside.

"What kind of jobs do we get to learn about in the garden?" Andy asked.

"How about exterminators?"

As usual, Cari needed a little time to learn a new long word. "What's an ex-term-i . . . I can't remember the rest of the word."

"Exterminators," Andy said. "Remember when the neighbors had carpenter ants eating into their wooden house?" Andy reminded his little sister. "They had a company come and spray to get rid of the problem. Those workers were exterminators."

"Oh." Cari thought for a moment. "Can animals carry bug spray?" she asked.

"They don't have to," Andy told her. "They just—just—hey, Dad, who are the forest exterminators, anyway?" Andy scratched his head. He couldn't think of any such animals.

Dad led them to a beautiful rosebush. He gently turned over a damp leaf. "Here's one of the smallest exterminators," he said.

"That's a ladybug," Cari cried. "Ladybug, ladybug, fly away home," she sang.

"Ladybugs eat insects that can harm flowers, fruit trees, and vegetables," Dad said. He put the leaf back in place.

"There's another ladybug." Cari stared at the lovely bright markings.

"Ladybugs aren't really bugs. They're members of the beetle family," Dad said. "Let's find some more exterminators." He led the children between some tall plants. "Andy, pull back the bottom leaves of that plant. Be careful."

Andy obeyed. "Hey, look!" Andy almost yelled. Then he remembered to squeeze the words into a whisper. A large toad peered up at them. "Are frogs exterminators?" Before he finished asking the question, the toad's long, sticky tongue darted out. It caught a flying insect and snapped it inside its large mouth.

"Toads and frogs eat insects, including flies," Dad said.

"Flies carry germs that make us sick."

Knowing that made Cari feel important. She wiggled with happiness.

The toad hopped beneath the leaves of another plant. Andy laughed. "It must like insects better than people. Any more exterminators, Dad?"

"There's one we see a lot," Dad said. "Let's see if I can locate one now." Dad walked toward the apple orchard. Cari trudged after him. She liked the *squeak, squeak* sound her boots made on the wet grass.

"There's an exterminator." Dad pointed to a spider's web. Heavy with raindrops, the web swayed from a branch.

Cari stepped back. "I don't like spiders. They're creepy."

"I like spiders," Andy boasted. "They eat more flies than anything. If God hadn't made spiders, there would be so many flies they would cover the whole world. Wouldn't they, Dad?"

"Maybe not that many flies," Dad said. "But spiders are a very useful part of life." He looked up at an enormous black cloud hurrying across the sky toward them. "Uh-oh! Looks like the rain's coming again. Time to get back inside and add exterminators to your list."

Cari and Andy raced for the house, and Dad raced right behind them. ●

7

Decorators

Cari sang a little song she made up. Dad and Mom and Andy said she was really smart. So she sang the song again: "Dad took us to the forest and to the yard. He showed us God's ex-ter-mi-na-tors. Ladybugs work hard. They eat insects that hurt our flowers and garden. Spiders and frogs and toads eat flies that have germs and make me sick. I am glad. When I'm sick, I feel sad."

Cari rushed to the window. The sun peeked at her through the clouds. She saw blue sky. "Dad, will you take us to the forest today?" she called.

"Let's wait until the grass is drier," Dad suggested.

"OK." Cari ran outside every five minutes, asking, "Is it dry enough now?" Finally Dad laughed and said they could go to the forest.

"The world had a bath," Cari said when they started out.

"No. A shower." Andy grinned. "See?" He pointed to the trees where water still dripped from the branches.

"The poor flowers," Cari said. The rain had caused most of the flowers to droop.

"They'll stand up again when they get dry," Dad promised.

Andy turned a cartwheel in the path. "I'm so glad to get out of the house again!" he sang out. Cari clapped her hands. When Andy turned rightside up, he asked, "What secret will we find today?"

"I think we'll look for the forest decorators." Dad carefully spread back some leaves and showed the children tiny blossoms hiding beneath. "Although God made flowers with nectar for birds and bees, one of the flowers' biggest jobs is to decorate the forest and make it beautiful."

Cari nodded and said, "Just like Mom decorated my room."

"Let's see how many different flowers we can find and how many colors."

"There's a field of yellow buttercups."

Andy pointed to hundreds of waxy, yellow flowers on short green stems.

Cari looked at the ground. "I see tiny pink flowers," she said.

"Those are wild geraniums," Dad told her.

"Bluebells," Andy called when he saw a clump of waving blossoms.

"Honeysuckle. Mmm, it smells good." Dad showed them delicate flowers growing on a vine over a broken-down fence.

"Purple violets!" Cari squealed.

"Columbine." Andy carefully tipped back a pale blue blossom with a white center.

"Wild currant." Dad pointed to a big bush with clusters of rosy red flowers.

"I wish I could find a trillium," Andy said. "But they bloom only in the spring."

"What's that?" Cari asked.

"A trillium is a beautiful flower, and it smells super," Andy explained. "Hey! I bet the *World Book* has pictures of trilliums and a lot of other flowers. We'll look when we go home."

A big raindrop *plunked* on Cari's nose. Dad grabbed her hand, and they raced for the house. Andy was right behind them. "Goodbye, forest decorators," Cari called.

After dinner the children got out the *World Book* and looked under "Flower." Cari smiled while looking at the pictures of colorful desert flowers and garden flowers. Then Andy said, "Here's a picture of a trillium listed under 'Flowers of Woodlands and Forests.'"

Cari looked at the pretty green leaves. She looked at the three shiny white petals that opened from a yellow center. "Tril-li-um. I like it best of all," she said. "When it's spring, can we find a trillium?"

"Of course," Dad promised. "It's one of my favorite flowers, too." He reached over and took Mom's hand. "You'll be well and strong long before the trilliums bloom."

She laughed. The skin around the corners of her blue eyes crinkled. "I'll be well and strong even before the autumn leaves fall! Today the doctor said I'm much better than he expected I'd be." She looked lovingly at her family. "Thanks to God and you."

"Mom, I can hardly wait for you to be able to go with us." Andy plopped down on the floor in front of her chair. She ruffled his thick hair with her fingers.

Cari climbed into Dad's lap and laid her head against his chest. "Thank you, Daddy, for taking us to the forest." She looked upward. "And thank You, God, for making all the pretty flowers, especially the trilliums." ●

Farmers

8

Farmers

Every time it rained, Cari and Andy got the *World Book* out and looked at the gorgeous colored pictures of flowers. Most of the time they barely remembered how disappointed they'd been that the family couldn't go on a trip this summer. Mom felt better every day. Dad never ran out of neat forest mysteries.

One day Dad and the children weeded their vegetable garden. Mom sat in a chair in the sun, just watching and resting. How glad they were to have her outside with them again!

Cari pulled out the plants her father said were weeds. At the end of a row she stopped and asked, "Dad, does the forest have farmers, like we're being today?"

"It sure does!" Dad pushed back his hat and smiled. He looked at his wristwatch and said, "We've done enough for now. Let's go see if we can find some of God's farmers."

"Great!" Andy shouted. He helped Cari up from the ground where she'd been sitting busily pulling up weeds.

The nodding trees and flowers seemed to welcome the explorers. The small animals that scurried by didn't act afraid. "That's because we stop, look, and listen," Cari whispered.

"So where are all the farmers?" Andy wanted to know.

"What's the first thing a farmer has to do?" Dad asked.

"Uh, dig up the ground." Andy looked at the upturned earth at his feet. "What did that?"

"A mole, maybe. Or a gopher. Earthworms also break up the ground by digging," Dad explained.

"I didn't know that." Cari bent down to examine the well-turned earth.

"Who does the planting?" Andy asked.

"The forest." Dad's blue eyes twinkled. "But there are helpers."

"Who? How?" the children asked together.

"Watch." Dad pointed to a big pine tree.

A gray squirrel with a cone in its mouth ran along a branch, then leaped to another. Just then a blue jay squawked. The squirrel dropped the cone, stopped, and chattered at the jay as if scolding the noisy bird. Then the squirrel raced on.

"The seeds in the cone will turn into tiny seedlings that grow to become big trees," Dad told the children. "Now look at that clump of dandelions."

Cari trotted over to the pretty yellow flowers. She liked them, even though they were pests when they got in the lawn. "Some are all white and puffy."

"They've gone to seed. Watch what happens."

A breeze blew against the dandelion puffs. Immediately they separated into hundreds of tiny, feather-like bits that sailed through the air.

"The wind is a farmer!" Cari shouted. She tried to catch the floating dandelion fluff, but it slipped through her fingers.

"So are the sun and the rain," Andy put in. He reached for an apple on a wild apple tree. "Is it OK to eat this, Dad?"

"If you want to. Wipe it on your jeans. No one has sprayed here."

"Want an apple, Cari?" She nodded yes, so Andy picked a small but juicy apple for her. Then he picked one for Dad. They all munched while walking. When they finished, they tossed the apple cores into the brush near the trail.

"Now we are planters," Dad teased the children. "The seeds from the cores will make new apple trees. Birds are planters too. They drop seeds."

"I'm a planter. Andy's a planter. Dad's a planter too," Cari sang. "That's neat!"

"Look at all the things I have to put on my list under 'Farmers,'" Andy bragged. "Moles and gophers and earthworms."

"Squirrels and dandelions," Cari chimed in. "Birds and us."

"Wind," Dad reminded the children. "Sun and rain."

"Don't forget snow." Andy grinned.

Cari thought for a moment. "Dad, how could God make all the forest farmers and everything?" She looked around the peaceful forest clearing.

"Just because He's God," Dad said quietly. "He loves us so much He wants us to have a beautiful world to live in."

"I'm glad!" Cari and Andy said at the same time. ●

9

Teachers

Mom." Cari snuggled into her mother's lap. "I get to go to school when summer is gone, don't I?"

Mom hugged her. "Yes, dear. You'll love going to school. You already know your letters and numbers. You can read simple words. Besides, Mrs. Swanson will be your teacher. She loves children."

"School will be so much fun." Cari wiggled herself into sitting straight. "Mom, does God have animal teachers?" Before Mom could answer, Cari rushed ahead to speak. "I really, really, really liked the farmers. Farmer animals broke up the ground. And the wind and rain are farmers too. And—" She ran out of breath.

"Yes, Cari. The forest community does have teachers. When Dad takes you and Andy for your stay-at-home forest walk today, maybe you will see some of God's forest teachers. Whew!" Mom laughed. "Now I'm out of breath too."

Cari found it hard to wait for lunchtime to be over so they could get started. "Mom, do you feel like going?" she asked.

"Not just yet—but soon," Mom promised. Mom's happiness made her face bright. "God has helped me so much."

"I'm glad!" Cari hugged her mother.

A few hours later Dad said, "Mom says you want to see some of God's teachers, Cari. Right?"

"Right!" both children answered.

"OK. We'll see what we can find. Remember, we have to be extra quiet. When animals and birds have their young with them, they frighten more easily. The larger animals such as bears and cougars—some people call them mountain lions—also become angry if you get near their babies.

"Never, ever get near a cub, such as a baby bear, cougar, or fox. Even if a cub *seems* to be alone, Mama Bear or Mama Cougar or Mama Fox is probably nearby. You'd be in *b-i-i-i-i-g* trouble. Animals fight to protect their young."

Dad looked so serious that Cari and Andy quickly promised to leave cubs alone.

"The best way to see forest teachers is to find a spot, settle down, and be patient." Dad led them to a little clearing where they could sit in the grass and lean back against a huge tree stump. Before long a lovely buck and doe (father and mother deer) stepped into the clearing. The buck had branching horns on his head. Andy whispered that the horns were antlers.

Cari put her hand over her mouth to keep from crying out when the two deer came closer. The next moment, two spotted fawns bounced into the open! They walked very close to the doe and did exactly what their mother did. Dad whispered, "The fawns are learning to be careful. See how they raise their heads and sniff?"

Cari watched the little family disappear into the forest. So the deer were teachers. "That's funny," she whispered to Andy. "They don't look at all like Mrs. Swanson." They both giggled softly.

That quiet afternoon the children saw mother birds showing their baby birds how to fly. The best thing of all happened on the way home. Andy pranced ahead but stopped. "Dad, here's a bird. The poor thing must have a broken wing."

Dad and Cari caught up with Andy, and Dad said, "That's a quail. She doesn't really have a broken wing. Stay here and watch." He stepped toward her. The quail dragged her wing and limped a few feet away. Dad followed. The quail did the same thing. Each time Dad came close, the quail went through the same actions.

Dad finally said, "It's all right, little quail. We won't hurt you or your babies." He motioned to Cari and Andy and said, "Come."

They obeyed. The mother quail limped ahead until they had gone a little way. Then she slid out of sight beneath the brush.

"Are you *sure* she wasn't hurt?" Cari asked.

"Yes, Cari." Dad squeezed her hand. "God created quail to protect their young by pretending to be hurt and leading intruders away from where they are hidden. We won't disturb them, but some place near, Mama Quail has a nest of young ones who have been taught not to make a peep. Her young are watching their mom's performance. When they are grown, they can do the same thing."

Cari thought of the beautiful, brave bird and nodded hard when Andy said, "She's the best teacher ever." ●

10

Landscapers

When they returned home, Cari and Andy talked and talked about the teachers they had seen when Dad took them to the forest. They praised the deer that taught their fawns to be careful and the birds that taught their little babies to fly. They talked most of all about the mama quail that faced danger by leading intruders away from the nest where her babies huddled.

"Did God have fun making all the animals and flowers and trees different?" Cari asked when she and Andy started out for another walk with Dad.

"Of course He did," Andy said. He stretched. He had been sleeping in the hammock between two big fir trees when Cari shouted, "Time to go!"

"I think He did too." Dad held Cari's small hand in his big hand. "Remember how we agreed all the animals are equally important? It's the same with people." He sighed. "If all people did what God created them to do, just as the forest community does, what a wonderful world it could be!"

"Dad." Cari clung to her father's hand. "God gets sad when people are naughty, right?"

"Of course He does," Andy put in. "That's how come He sent Jesus, so we could believe on Him and do what we're supposed to do. Dad, at church school our teacher said no matter how beautiful it is here on earth, heaven is so much better we can't even *think* how great it is. Really and truly, Dad?"

"Really and truly, Andy. The Bible says so."

Cari looked up at the bright blue sky. She looked at the patches of sunlight and shade, the big trees and small flowers. She heard many birds singing and felt the soft moss brush against her feet as she walked along in her sandals. How could anything be better? "I love Jesus," she said. "Someday I'll live with Him in heaven, won't I, Dad?"

"Of course. That's what knowing, loving, and serving Jesus is all about. He may come in a little while, or He may wait a longer time. It doesn't really matter. When Jesus returns to earth, He will take all of us who love and serve Him to His home. We'll be with Him forever."

Andy hopped over a dead branch in the trail. He picked it up and threw it aside so that Cari wouldn't trip. "How long is forever?" she asked.

"Forever never ends," Dad said.

Cari didn't understand what that meant, but she said, "If Jesus is there and all my family is there, I'm glad heaven won't ever end."

"That's my girl!" Dad patted her curly hair.

They reached the same clearing where they had seen the deer family the day before. "Can we sit by the stump and see if they'll come back?" Cari asked. Dad nodded yes. Soon a little brown rabbit hopped out of the bushes. Cari watched it nibble grass. "Dad, the deer and bunnies are so adorable! But what's their forest job?" she whispered.

"The bunny is working now," Dad said in a mysterious voice.

"All it's doing is eating grass," Cari said. "That's what the deer did, too."

"I know!" Andy kept his voice low. His eyes sparkled like two blue lakes in the sun.

"They're landscapers. You know, groundskeepers. Hey, Dad, why can't we get some deer and rabbits? They'd keep our grass cut better than a lawn mower!"

Cari giggled. The rabbit's head shot up. It moved to another patch of grass, keeping its long ears turned up and twitching its nose.

"Cows eat grass too," Andy went on. "Horses and donkeys and—"

"Buffaloes!" Cari interrupted him.

"Where did you see a buffalo?" A smile tugged at Andy's lips. "We sure don't have any buffaloes around Darrington."

"In the *World Book*," Cari answered. "Buffaloes are all shaggy and have big fronts and little backs!"

Andy laughed so loud a frightened rabbit leaped up and ran across the clearing.

"Books are wonderful," Dad said. "This winter we'll study a lot about forests and animals, but mostly about God and Jesus. All right?"

"All right," Andy said. Cari smiled and shouted, "I feel good all over!" ●

11

Utilities and Welfare

C ari watched Andy working on the big list of forest secrets they had seen during their stay-at-home vacation. "It's getting long," Cari said.

Andy looked up. "It sure is." He held up one hand, which had red and blue and green ink from his marker pens. "Glad this stuff washes off. I look like a rainbow!"

Cari giggled. "I'm glad you printed the letters," she told him. "It helps me to learn to read."

Dad and Mom looked at Andy's list. "What a lovely poster your list would make," they said.

"Yeah." He smiled. When they left the room, he whispered, "Cari, can you keep a secret? A big, huge, enormous secret." He sounded so mysterious, Cari shivered.

"I promise," she said.

"I'm going to make Mom a poster for a get-well present." His face shone. "I'll put everything we've learned on it. After we discover a bunch more forest secrets, I'll make another poster."

Cari decided to color a picture for her mother. Andy helped her trace flower pictures from the *World Book*. She colored inside the lines so well Andy said even he couldn't have done better! Cari saved her flower picture until Andy's poster was ready. He worked really hard.

When Andy's poster was done, it looked like this:

THE FOREST COMMUNITY

Builders
birds
beavers

Bankers
squirrels
chipmunks

Supermarket

berries	twigs
nuts	roots
corn	water lilies
seeds	nectar
bark	grubs

mushrooms   lichens

Garbage Collectors
coyotes
wolves
buzzards

Doctors, Nurses, Pharmacy
| ants | foxglove |
| grass | dock |

Exterminators
| ladybugs | frogs |
| toads | spiders |

Decorators
buttercups	honeysuckle
wild geraniums	wild currant
bluebells	
columbine	trilliums

Farmers
moles	dandelions
gophers	wind
earthworms	sun
squirrels	rain
birds	snow
cones	people

Teachers

deer	quail

Landscapers

rabbits	horses
deer	donkeys
cows	buffaloes

"Why, children!" Mom looked and looked at her picture and her poster. "These are so beautiful. Thank you very much."

Andy and Cari felt great. They felt even better when Dad mysteriously said, "We have a surprise for you, too." He wouldn't say anything more until they finished lunch. "Get ready for your nature walk," he told them. When they came out to the porch, there stood Mom, all ready to go with them! She looked strong and healthy, not sick, as she had been for so long.

"What are you going to show us today?" she asked Dad. Happiness danced in her eyes.

"I think we'll talk about utilities and welfare today. They're an important part of the forest community."

"Lightning makes electricity." Andy turned a cartwheel to show how happy he was. "The sun makes light. So do the moon and the stars, at night, I mean."

"The sun gives heat." Cari held her arm out and felt it get warm.

"Snow also gives heat," Dad said. "It acts like the blankets on your bed."

"*I* like the creeks and rivers and ponds and lakes," Cari said. "They give water." She laughed, and the little stream seemed to chuckle with her.

"Light, heat, water. They're utilities," Andy said. "But what's welfare?"

"Welfare is seeing there is shelter available. See if you can find animal shelters."

Cari noticed her friend, the little brown bunny, hop under some bushes. "Bushes," she whispered.

"Trees," Andy added when a squirrel disappeared into a hole in a big tree.

"I see something else." Cari raced to peek into a small hollowed-out cave under an overhanging dirt bank. "When it snows, this will be a good animal hotel," she said.

"Yeah," Andy agreed. He squirmed down a sloping clay bank and peered into a hole beneath the great roots of a tree that had been torn from the ground by a storm. "Here's another. I bet this hole stays dry even when it rains hard. God sure makes good animal shelters." ●

Forest Police

12

Forest Police

"It's so neat having Mom feel good enough to go into the forest with us," Andy told Cari.

"Even though we didn't get to go on a trip this summer, we had fun," Cari said. "Besides, Dad says we can learn neat things about what God made all year, not just in the summer."

"Yeah." Andy grinned.

Cari smiled too. She loved her brother, who was twice as old as she was. Now she climbed onto his lap and hugged him.

He ruffled her hair and gave her a pat. "Get your shoes on, Cari. It's almost time to go," Andy told her.

Just before they left, the wail of a siren

split the quiet country air. A police car went dashing by. Cari asked, "Dad, are there police in the forest community?"

"There are many, many. I'll show you some. We'll find more in the *World Book* tonight, if you like," he promised.

Sure enough, after they reached the cool, shady area under the big evergreen trees, Dad began to point out all kinds of wonderful things.

"God gave different animals and insects different ways of protection," he said. "Look."

Cari's eyes opened wide. A tiny gopher sat as still as a stick by a hole in the ground. When Cari moved, *whoosh!* The gopher dashed down into the hole. *Whoosh! Whoosh!* Other gophers Cari hadn't even seen raced to the hole and popped down. "Hey! The first gopher must have been a guard."

"Pretty good guard, I'd say." Andy stared into the hole but couldn't see the gophers. Dad said the gophers had escaped through their emergency escape tunnels.

A little later Andy wrinkled his nose. "Yeccch, I smell a skunk. Phew!" He held his nose and made a horrible face.

"God gave skunks that odor for protection," Dad said. "Now look over there."

Cari tilted her head back. Across the little clearing, a flock of birds screamed.

"What's happening?"

"See the hawk?" Dad said. "It must have tried to attack a smaller bird. Look at all the other birds dive-bombing the hawk to drive it off."

"Wow, one bird's acting as a decoy and leading it away," Andy yelled out. "Go on, you old hawk. Leave the other birds alone!" Either Andy's yelling or the dive-bombing flock did the trick. The huge hawk gave up the battle and quickly flew away.

"God has given other ways of warning," Dad said. "If you ever accidentally step on a yellow jacket, get out of there fast! A yellow jacket's body is created so that when it gets hurt, it gives off an odor. That signals its fellow wasps. They come and attack in force."

That evening Cari and Andy and their parents studied about some other forest police. They learned a lot of super things God did when He created all of life. Cari and Andy especially enjoyed learning these three facts:

1. Termites that love damp wood have soldiers whose only job is to defend the termite colony. They use their powerful jaws and strong legs, usually against invading ants. The soldiers are blind and wingless.

They must be fed and groomed by the worker termites.

2. Ants sting and bite and tap the walls of their nests to warn their community of danger. Some ants make squeaky or buzzing sounds. Others release chemicals that spell out danger.

3. Although fireflies in the western United States don't give off light, those elsewhere do. Andy laughed and called them "nature's night patrol."

"What a lot of things we have to add to our forest community list," Cari said after family devotions. "Andy, you'll have to . . ." Andy shook his head to remind Cari the poster was supposed to be their secret. Cari decided to ask a question instead.

"Mom, if God cares enough to do all those things for bugs and animals, He must love me a whole lot. Right?"

"Enough to send Jesus so you can love Him and live with Him forever," Mom told her.

Cari nodded. "I love Jesus. God too." ●

13

Weather Forecasters

What's the weather forecast?" Dad asked one evening.

"I know," Cari shouted. "Sunny and warm."

"Good. That means we can have another nature walk tomorrow." Dad's eyes twinkled in the same way that Cari's and Andy's eyes did. He took a deep breath.

"I sure didn't know ants and termites and bees and skunks and gophers and fireflies and birds act as forest police until you told us last time, Dad." Andy's freckles stood out like shiny, new pennies. In the sunshine, he looked like he had more freckles.

"The forest doesn't have weathermen," Andy said.

"Or weatherwomen." Mom grinned.

Dad raised one eyebrow. "Oh, but God definitely built weather forecasting into His forest community. It may take longer to show you how it works, especially since it's sunny and warm, but just wait," he teased.

A few days later when the Reynolds family started home from their nature walk, clouds gathered above them.

"Is there going to be a storm?" Cari looked at the rolling clouds.

"Let's find out from our animal weather forecasters," Dad told her. "Stop, look, and listen."

After a few moments Andy complained, "There isn't anything to see—or hear. Everything is still, like the forest is kind of waiting."

"Why aren't the birds singing?" Cari listened carefully. She noticed a small rabbit scurry into a hollow log. A squirrel zipped up a tree trunk and vanished into its nest. It didn't even take time to chatter and scold, the way it usually did.

"I see a bird," Andy announced and pointed. "It isn't flying or singing. Does the bird know there's going to be a storm?"

Cari looked at the bird all huddled beneath a clump of bushes with its head under its wing. "It must know. The rabbit, too, and the squirrel."

"God created a lot of knowledge in His animals," Dad told them. "Remember when I said you would have to wait to discover the forest weather forecasters? Now we'd better hurry to our home. That storm is getting closer all the time."

Black clouds scowled harder and harder. A faint boom in the distance told them thunder was on its way. They barely made it home before the storm hit. At the window of their cozy house, they watched the hail mixed with rain. Thunder boomed and lightning flashed. After the storm moved on, the Reynolds family talked about forest forecasters.

"I know a great big animal that's smart about weather," Andy boasted. "It's furry and sleeps a lot."

Cari clapped her hands. "A bear!" She wrinkled her nose and tilted her head to one side. "Mom, you tell me when it's time to go to bed. How do bears know when to hi-bear-nate?"

"Not hi-*bear*-nate. The word is hi-*ber*-nate," Mom explained.

"You can remember that because bears sleep in the winter when it's cold. Cold makes us say *brrrr*."

"OK, but how do they know?" Cari asked.

"God created a kind of alarm clock in bears," Dad said. "It doesn't ring, but bears know in the fall when it's time to eat everything they can find. They have to put on enough fat to nourish them until spring." He laughed. "There's nothing crosser than a bear who gets awakened before it finishes its long winter nap!"

"Nothing except me when I have to get up early," Andy added.

"Look, the rain has stopped." Cari ran to the door. "The sun is coming out."

Andy followed her to the big porch. "Wow! There must be a gazillion robins on the lawn!"

Cari stared at the red-breasted birds. "Andy, what are they doing?" She pointed to a large robin with its head cocked to one side. The next instant it dug its beak into the rain-softened ground and came up with a long angleworm! Other robins did the same.

"They're listening," Andy told her.

A robin flew to the low branch of a nearby tree and began singing.

"That's neat," Cari said when other robins joined in. "On our next walk can we see if God has a forest choir?"

"Of course," her parents said at the same time.

The family listened to the sweet music for a long time. At last, evening came, and the robins flew away for the night. But long after they were gone, Cari and Andy talked about how smart the robins were and how beautifully they sang. ●

14

God's Forest Choir

"Want to hear a really old joke?" Andy asked Cari.

"Sure," Cari said. She liked her brother's jokes, even his old ones.

"This joke is a riddle," Andy said. "That means I ask you a question, and you try to guess the answer."

"OK."

"Why do bees hum?" Mischief danced in Andy's eyes.

Cari thought and thought. She remembered all the times she'd heard bees humming in the sunshine. "Because they want to?" she finally asked.

Andy shook his head. "Guess again."

"I can't, Andy. Why do they hum?"

"Because they don't know the words to the songs!"

Cari giggled. "Yeah. They don't know the words." Cari ran to tell Mom and Dad Andy's joke. Then she asked, "May we go to the forest now?"

"For a little while," Mom said.

Soon they crawled under the barbed-wire fence. It separated their property from the trail leading across the field and down to the woods, Dan's Creek, and the Sauk River. Andy raced ahead. Cari trotted right behind him.

"Hey, you two," Dad called. "How do you expect to see and hear things when you make all that racket by running?"

"Sorry, Dad. We forgot to stop, look, and listen." Andy slowed down.

So did Cari. "Hey, Dad," Cari said. "When will I hear God's forest choir?"

Dad led the way to their favorite stump in the clearing. They sat in the grass and closed their eyes. Bees hummed in a patch of clover. Remembering Andy's joke, Cari whispered, "They don't know the words."

Bird calls and songs came from thickets and trees. Insects buzzed in the grass.

Andy whispered, "Listen to the big bass drum."

Thrum. Thrum. Thrum.

"What is it?" Cari asked.

"A grouse or pheasant is drumming with its wings. God has an orchestra in His forest, as well as a choir," Dad said in a low voice.

"Brrrrrscreeeee. Brrrrrscreeeee."

"I know what makes that noise—a squirrel." Cari quickly turned toward a big maple tree. Sure enough, a chattery squirrel sat watching them from a branch.

Chirp. Chirp. "What's that?" Andy wanted to know.

"Crickets. They rub their wings together to make that sound," Dad answered.

A shadow fell over the ground, followed by a harsh *Caw! Caw! Caw! Caw!*

"Crows." Andy laughed. "I bet they think they've got the best voices in God's choir, even when all they can do is caw."

"Maybe blue jays think they're the best," Cari guessed. She put her hands over her ears to shut out the screams of two noisy jays that took flight.

Che-runk! Cher-unk!

"There's the one who sings bass, the real low singing part," Andy said. He pointed to a huge frog sitting on a lily pad.

"In the spring you'll hear little peeper frogs singing by lakes and ponds," Mom promised. "I always feel spring is really here when the peepers sing."

"How could God think of so many ways for the forest creatures to sing?" Cari sat down on a fallen log and listened to the different birds and animals praising God in their own ways.

"God is so powerful that He knows and can do everything," Dad said.

"What if He got mixed up?" Cari asked. "It sure would be funny if a frog screeched like a blue jay!"

"Or a rabbit howled like a coyote." Dad laughed at the idea.

"Or a bee bellowed like a bull." Andy turned a handspring and came up with his hair sticking out every which way.

"Or a squirrel chirped like a cricket," Mom put in.

"Or a crow sang like a robin." Andy liked the silly game. "It couldn't really happen, though. God never makes mistakes."

"God knows what fits best. Even when we can't see why He does certain things, we still know He knows best," Dad said.

Cari lay in the soft grass. She looked at the blue sky, waving tree branches, and blooming flowers. She listened to the forest choir sing. She said, "I'm glad God made everything 'xackly the way it is." Then she looked and listened some more. ●

Firefighters

15

Firefighters

Mom, Cari, and Andy stood on the big covered front porch of their home. Across the road, tall timber and low hills grew until a small mountain covered with trees rose in front of them.

Boom! Crash! Bang! The loud thunder made the windows of their house rattle. Big storm-tossed clouds raced by.

Cari slipped closer to Mom. "I—I don't like thunder." She shivered, and Mom hugged the little girl.

"I love thunder." Andy hollered above the *Boom! Crash! Bang!*

Cari was almost in tears. "Lightning sets fires in the woods," she sobbed. "Dad can't come home until the fires go out."

Mom sighed. "No, dear, he can't."

"He's been gone so long." Cari sighed. "I want him to come home."

"I do too, Cari. But he has to work until the fires are put out. Loggers are pulled off their jobs to fight fire."

A brilliant flash of lightning made the gray day bright for a moment.

"This is a good time to play I Spy," Mom told the children.

Even Andy looked interested. He liked to play games just as much as Cari did.

Mom pointed to the little mountain where tiny wisps of white smoke had started to rise. "Look. The lightning has set trees on fire on Gold Hill. As soon as the lightning flashes, we'll look carefully. Whoever sees where a new fire is set says 'I spy.'"

"I spy!" Andy yelled. He pointed to the right side of Gold Hill where a new fire sent a little smoke signal up into the air.

During the next half hour Andy, Cari, and Mom spied more than 30 fires that had been set by one lightning storm.

"Guess what, Mom? I'm not scared anymore," Cari said.

"Good," Mom answered. "I always find a storm interesting, but pray it doesn't do damage."

The lightning moved on, and the thunder chased after it.

"I guess our game is over," Andy said. "It was so exciting! There goes the fire truck!" He ran to the end of the gravel driveway in front of the house, but stayed well back from the road. After the truck passed, he trotted back to the porch.

"The firefighters will try to put out all those fires," Mom said. "It's a good thing they'll have God's firefighters to help them."

"Does God have forest firefighters?" Cari looked surprised.

"Sure. The best ones are starting to work now." Andy pointed to the sheets of rain that had begun pouring from the black skies just after he reached the porch.

"Raindrops are firefighters." Cari jumped up and down. "They work together, like Dad and his friends, don't they?"

Mom nodded. The rain swept away the hot air that had made them feel as though they would melt. One by one the white wisps of smoke disappeared. The fire-fighting raindrops had drowned every fire.

Dad came home that night. He was covered with black soot and smelled like a campfire. He was more tired than his children had ever seen him. "We thanked God for the rain," he said. "There were so many fires! We wondered if we would be able to control them." He yawned. "I need a bath and bed."

The next day Dad talked about the fire. "While I was gone, I saw something I will probably never see again. I saw one of the most mysterious secrets of the forest."

"Really, Dad?" Andy moved closer to Dad. Cari and Mom moved closer to Dad so they could hear every word.

"Someone at our camp carelessly dropped a match that wasn't all the way out," Dad said. He frowned. "I started to stamp out the flame. Then I noticed the match had fallen on an anthill. I stooped to grab the match, but a force of ants beat me to it. They rushed to the match and released fluid from their bodies to put out the fire."

"All right!" Andy shouted. "Nobody but God could have thought of fire-fighting ants!" ●

16

Pilots

When I grow up, I'm going to be a pilot," Andy said. *"Vroom! Vroom!"* He waved his arms, dipped his body, and ran past Cari.

She jumped from the bottom porch step and followed him. *"Vroom! Vroom! This is fun."* She waved her arms and followed Andy.

"There are a lot of pilots in God's forest community," Andy said. "Crows and robins . . ."

"Swallows and bluebirds," Cari added to the list.

"Hawks and starlings and wrens and snowbirds," Andy put in.

"Blue jays and—and—" Cari couldn't think of any more birds.

"The next time Dad takes us to the forest, Cari, let's see how many bird pilots we can see." Andy stopped pretending to be a pilot. "I must add some more groups of forest secrets to my list so I can make another poster sometime."

Cari helped Andy remember the many things they had learned. He mumbled while he wrote them down. "Sun, moon, and stars make light. Creeks and rivers and lakes and ponds have water. Sun and snow give heat. Bushes and holes and caves offer shelter."

Cari tried to remember more secrets Dad had taught them on their stay-at-home vacation nature walks. "Don't forget the forest police: birds and ants and termites. Remember how God made animals and birds know when storms are coming."

Andy wrote faster. "Remember all the creatures who sing and croak in God's forest choir and His orchestra." Andy quickly listed frogs and crickets, birds, and other animals.

Cari thought of the big thunder-and-lightning storm. Andy wrote *rain* and *ants* under the "Firefighter" heading. Last of all, he wrote "Pilots" and listed all kinds of birds and flying insects.

A few days later their nature walk led them up a steep hill. Cari and Andy were panting by the time they dragged themselves to the big rock at the top of the hill. Mom was tired too, but Dad was used to climbing on his logging job.

"If we're lucky, we might see an eagle," Dad told them. The family sat quietly for a long, long time. They were glad to rest before walking downhill. Then they spied an enormous bird with powerful wings floating above them. It circled, glided, and circled twice more before giving a lonely cry and flying away.

"I am so glad the United States chose the eagle as its national bird," Mom told Dad. She watched the eagle until it disappeared in the distance. "The eagle stands for freedom."

"The Bible says if our country or any country will follow Him, they shall be under His protection,"* Dad said. He looked at his watch. "We'd better go. It's a long walk home."

On the way down the hill, he told them more about the eagle. "When it's time for the baby birds—called eaglets—to fly, their mother is right there with them. It takes time for them to learn. They stay close to the nest at first. The wonderful thing is, if an eaglet flaps its wings but is too weak to fly, the mother eagle dives underneath the falling eaglet, catches it on her powerful wing, and brings it back to safety."

"Just like Jesus," Andy said.

"Really?" Cari opened her eyes wide—and her ears. She wanted to hear how an eagle could be like Jesus.

Andy knew what he said was true. He explained, "When Jesus sees us getting into trouble, He helps us. I mean, if we ask Him. Right, Dad?"

"Yes, He does, son. We have to remember one thing, though. We must never deliberately do things we know will get us into trouble and then expect Jesus to get us out of our mess. We can depend on Him, but He wants us to become strong, just as the eaglets become strong when they learn to fly on their own. God is always with us if we let Him be, but it's up to us to be where He wants us."

Just before they got home the eagle flew high above them. Cari and Andy waved to the graceful bird and wondered if a tiny eaglet might be riding on its mother's wing. ●

*2 Chronicles 7:14

17

Travelers

Dad looked ready to burst with excitement. "I have a few days off from work," he said. "Some of our logging equipment must be repaired. Do you want to take a short vacation?"

Mom gave a little shout of happiness. "That would be wonderful! It's been so long since we went away for a few days."

"Hurrah!" yelled Andy and Cari. They grabbed Dad around his knees and legs. "Will we fly like the birds who are pilots in God's forest community?" Andy asked.

"No, I think we'll travel by car," Dad said. "Since we live with mountains all around us, don't you think it would be nice to go to the beach on the coast?"

"Yes!" the children shouted.

The family quickly packed what they would need on their vacation. Andy told Cari, "I really like all the forest stuff Dad showed us on our walks, but just wait until you see the beach. It is so cool." He laughed hard. "The water is a whole lot more than cool. It makes me shiver just to remember how cold the Pacific Ocean is!"

"Have I been to the ocean, Andy?" Cari wrinkled her face as she tried to remember.

"You went so long ago you were probably too little to remember." Andy shoved his swimsuit and a huge towel into his suitcase. "You're going to love the ocean, Cari."

When they arrived at the ocean, Cari asked, "Where does it stop? The water goes right up into the sky." Andy had to explain that because they could see so far with no hills or mountains in the way, it just looked as if the sky and water were part of each other.

Cari had a great time playing in the warm sand, rolling a beach ball, and wading in the water. She always held tightly to Mom's or Dad's hand when they went wading. Andy wasn't allowed to go out very far into the water. The cold water and foam tickled their toes and made them laugh and shiver.

"It smells funny here," Cari said.

"That's because there's so much salt in the ocean," Andy said. He picked up a big piece of kelp and snapped it on the beach. He dodged out of the way of a crab scuttling across the sand.

Cari liked the sand dollars. The whole family laughed at skinny-legged birds that raced up and down the beach and at the seagulls that cried and begged for scraps from their lunches.

One of the most interesting things at the beach was learning about the odd creatures that lived there. "Hermit crabs are travelers," Dad said. "They live in empty seashells. When they get too big for their houses, they just find bigger and better homes."

"Kind of like us, Dad?" Andy asked.

Dad looked puzzled. "I'm not sure just what you mean."

"Well, someday when we get through living here, we'll go to a bigger and better home in heaven." Andy added a little more damp sand to the sand castle he was building.

"You're right," Dad said.

Several days passed. The family packed their belongings, told the beach and ocean goodbye, and started the long drive home to Darrington.

"I can't wait to get home!" Andy said. "I had fun, but home . . . well, home is home."

He thought for several minutes and then asked, "Did God put something inside us that makes us want to go home?"

"I've always felt that He did." Mom spoke quietly. "Long before America became the United States, the Native Americans traveled a lot, searching for food. Many tribes, however, had a home camp, a permanent place to which they could return."

Andy sat as far forward in his seat as his seat belt would allow him to. "Geese and swallows go south for the winter, but they go home in the spring or summer," he said. "They return to some places on the very same day every year."

"There are also many true stories of pets who find their way home," Dad told them.

Cari caught sight of the white house waiting patiently for its family. Sunlight gleamed on the front windows. "Look, Andy, our house is smiling at us," she cried. "Hi, house! We're home!" ●

18

Collectors

"Cari, are you ready?" Andy called from the porch.

"Almost." She finished tying her shoes and ran to join her family. They were going to see more things God had created in His forest community.

On their way across the field dotted with stumps, Cari and Andy found pretty rocks and bits of wood. Soon their pockets bulged. "We're collectors." Andy grinned.

"You remind me of some lines from a poem," Mom teased.

"Please, say the words, Mom." Cari grabbed her mother's hand and swung it.

Mom quoted:

Collectors

"'Then we gather, as we travel, bits of
    moss and dirty gravel,
And we chip off little specimens of
    stone;
And we carry home as prizes funny
    bugs of handy sizes
Just to give the day a scientific
    tone.'"*

"That's funny!" Andy laughed.

Cari laughed too. Then she asked, "What are specimens and scientific?"

"*Specimens* are samples. *Scientific* comes from a word that means to have knowledge or know things through studying."

Cari skipped to Dad's side and asked, "Dad, did God make forest collectors?"

"Oh, yes." Dad laughed hard. "Do you remember my telling you about the big birds we call camp robbers? People who work in the woods don't dare turn their backs on their lunches. If they do, they're liable to turn around in time to see a sandwich go flying through the air in a camp robber's beak!"

Mom and the children laughed. "I can almost see a big bird grabbing Dad's sandwich and carrying it away," Cari said.

"I don't think the camp robber collects. He just eats," Andy protested. "Aren't there any real collectors in the forest?"

"Let's sit down here in the clearing, and I'll tell you a story," Dad suggested.

"Goody!" Cari said. She and Andy plopped down in the grass.

"A long time ago I had to stay in a bunkhouse at camp because my job was too far away from home to go back and forth on the crew bus every day. Something happened I will never forget."

"What's a bunkhouse?" Cari asked.

"A bunkhouse is a big building with lots of beds for the workingmen to sleep in."

"What happened, Dad?"

"We all liked one another and got along fine until some of our belongings started disappearing!"

"Really?" Andy sat straight up. "Was one of the loggers a thief?"

"That's what we didn't know," Dad said. "First, someone complained that his pen was missing. We thought he might have mislaid it. Then another pen disappeared. Almost every day someone discovered something was missing. Finally, a valuable watch vanished."

"Oh, no! What did you *do*?" Andy leaned forward and held his breath.

"No one confessed. So I decided to keep watch. It wasn't easy. You know how tired

I am after working all day. I felt my eyelids drooping. I tried hard to stay awake. Everyone else had fallen asleep a long time ago. Then I heard a scuffling sound. I opened my eyes. Moonlight shone in through the open bunkhouse window—"

"What was it?" Cari cried.

"The thief was heading for the window! A big pack rat had something shiny in its mouth."

"Really?" squeaked the children.

"Really." Dad's eyes sparkled. "I slid from my bunk and tiptoed outside. I followed the thief to its nest and found—"

"Pens!" Cari shouted.

"The watch!" Andy yelled.

"Yes. We were all glad none of the men had stolen those things. That day we put up a strong screen to keep the robber out."

"Something similar happened when I was teaching school," Mom added. "We found our thief when a pet crow owned by one of the boys flew right into the room and snatched a pencil."

"God doesn't want us to steal," Andy said. "But I guess birds and animals don't know any better. They are real collectors." ●

---

*Charles Edward Carryl, "Robinson Crusoe's Story"

19

Fishers

I don't have to go to work tomorrow," Dad announced. "Are you tired of animals? Have we seen a lot of them this summer?"

"Oh, no!" they answered. "We love animals!"

Dad's blue eyes twinkled. "How would you like to visit a very special place tomorrow? We'll see many animals you probably won't ever see in the woods. They are shy around people."

"Are we going to the Woodland Park Zoo in Seattle?" Mom asked. She looked as excited as the children. Mom was so happy to be able to travel with her family since God helped make her well.

"No. None of us have been to this place.

Some of the men I work with told me about it. They say it's a great place to visit. On the way to Mount Rainier there's a large forest area called Northwest Trek. I thought we could take a picnic lunch and spend the day there." His eyes twinkled again. "Maybe we'll see some fishers."

"You mean fishermen?" Andy tried not to sound disappointed. Who cared about seeing fishermen? Almost every time they went to the Sauk River someone stood casting a line into the water, trying to catch a fish.

"Not fisher*men. Fishers* . . . from the forest community. Now, who wants to go?"

"I do!" Cari raised her hand. So did Mom and Andy.

"Pack pajamas and toothbrushes," Dad said. "We'll stay in a motel overnight and go to Mount Rainier the next day."

It took about three hours to drive from Darrington to Northwest Trek near Eatonville. The family had fun playing car games on the way. Once inside the park, they quickly ate their lunch so they could get in line. An hour-long tram car ride took them past lakes and ponds and through meadows dotted with trees. Andy borrowed a pencil and a piece of paper from Mom. He wrote this list of what they saw on their tram ride: swans, ducks, crows, pigeons, bison, deer, elk, caribou, raccoons, Rocky Mountain goats, bighorn sheep, and pronghorn antelope.

Some of the animals had babies with them. The Reynolds family saw baby goats and woolly lambs, one baby antelope, and many baby bison or buffalo. One mother bison—buffalo—nursed her baby right by the tram road.

"I love it!" Cari cried out every time they saw something new.

When they got off the tram, Dad asked, "How many fishers did you see?"

"Ducks and raccoons," Andy answered. "Will we see some more animals?"

"Yes," Dad said. "There's a whole area for us to walk through." He led them up a paved trail to some overlooks. These were places where they could look across water and rocks into the forest.

"Kittens!" Cari squealed and pointed.

"No. Those are lynx cubs with their parents, Cari," Dad explained. Cari loved watching the cubs tumble and play together. Next the family saw cougars and bobcats.

Then they came to a rocky area that looked down on several large wolves and a bear.

"That bear is a fisher," Andy told Cari. When they got to the special forest animals area, they saw wolverines. "Dad, these wolverines don't look so fierce," Andy said. One wolverine lay asleep in a hollow log. Another one was asleep in a shady corner.

They saw a badger walking back and forth, like a soldier on guard duty. They also spotted two busy beavers gnawing trees by their pond.

Dad told them the two river otters were also fishers. The otters used a hollowed-out log for a slide into the water. The family even saw a animal called a "fisher." "That's the animal's nickname," Dad said. "It's really a marten. It eats rodents, including porcupines, but not fish."

"Yecch!" Andy made a horrible face. Cari did too.

The next day as they traveled homeward from Mount Rainier, Dad said, "Remember how Jesus told His disciples to fish for other people, not fish? That means we are to share the good news that Jesus loves us."

"I'd rather be that kind of fisher," Cari said. She yawned. "I'd hate to eat raw fish like the forest fishers do!"

Her family agreed with her. ●

20

Guides

Summer was nearly over. Cari and Andy hated that their trips would have to end. Dad and Mom had taught them so many things about God's forest community and other nature places. The children had learned that God created plants and animals and birds and insects and that each did different things.

One afternoon a loud *honk, honk* told the children Dad had come home a little early from his work in the woods.

"Come on, Cari!" Andy called out and raced outside to meet Dad. "Maybe there's time for another nature walk before it gets dark." Now that the weather had grown cooler, Dad no longer went to work super early or came home at lunchtime. The exploring trips had to be taken after supper.

After a quick meal, Dad, Mom, Cari, and Andy headed across the fields and down to the river. "Fall is coming." Mom pointed to dry, brown ferns and yellow leaves on the maple and cottonwood trees.

Soon it would get dark earlier and the family would go for walks only on the weekends. Each week more leaves turned yellow. Vine maple and sumac changed to bright red and orange. Mornings felt crisp and tingly. One afternoon the loud honking didn't come from Dad's car or the crew bus. It came from a large band of wild geese flying south for the winter. They looked like a giant flat V in the sky.

"Are the forest travelers playing follow the leader?" Cari asked.

"At school we learned that one goose serves as a guide and leads for a while. When it gets tired, it drops back and another goose takes its turn," Andy told her.

The honking stopped, and the flying geese disappeared.

Cari looked sad, but Mom hugged her. "They'll be back in the spring. How about asking Dad for information about God's forest guides, after supper tonight?"

"OK." Cari brightened up and helped

set the table for Mom. Andy stirred the spaghetti sauce, which smelled so good.

"Tell us about the forest guides, please, Dad," Andy said later. "I know that in the olden days the pioneers had guides." Cari climbed into Dad's lap and waited.

"Wolves travel in packs and have a leader," Dad said. "Wild horses are led by stallions that are always strong and smart enough to help keep their herd from danger."

Dad grinned. "Ever hear about the bee scouts?"

"You mean Boy Scouts, like I'll be pretty soon?" Andy asked.

"No, *bee* scouts."

"Are you teasing?" Mom asked.

"Not at all. One of the most interesting and mysterious things in all of God's nature creation is the bee scouts' waggle dance."

"What's that?" Cari squirmed.

"Bee scouts are called 'foragers,' because they forage or search to find food. When a bee scout finds a source of nectar or pollen, she flies back to the hive. She actually dances, either at the entrance or on the combs inside. This performance is called a waggle dance because of the way the bee wags her body. The way the bee scout dances depends on how far away the food is and in which direction and whether the scout flew with or against the wind."

"Why, Dad?" Andy wanted to know.

"If the food is far away, the other bees must know how far so they can take enough honey with them to have energy for the journey. A bee colony leaves the old hive for a new one only after the bee scouts have found a new nesting site." Andy and Cari thought about the bee scouts for a long time.

At the beginning of the summer the children could not have guessed how many things God had put into His forest community. "Are there still more things to see in the forest?" Cari asked.

Dad nodded yes.

Andy looked serious. "The geese follow their leader. So do wild horses and wolves, even bees. We follow Jesus because He's our leader. Right?"

"Yes, Andy," Mom answered.

"I'm glad," Andy said. A grin spread all over Andy's face when he said, "God's the best guide of all." ●

21

Timekeepers

Cari pressed her nose against the front-room window. "Here comes Dad," she called. "Come on, Andy!" Cari flung the door open and raced across the porch, down the steps, and onto the pine-needle path. She stopped at the edge of the road and waited while Dad swung down the steps of the big old crew bus.

"Good night, Bill. Take care of that foot," the bus driver called out as Dad hobbled off the road.

Andy rushed past Cari and put his arm around Dad's waist. "Lean on me, Dad."

"I'll carry your lunch bucket," Cari offered.

"Thanks. I can use some help." Dad

tried to smile. Big drops of sweat came to his forehead. He looked pale. He handed his lunch bucket to Cari and draped one of his arms over Andy's shoulders.

"What happened?" Andy wanted to know.

"I'll tell you when we get inside." Dad rested some of his weight on Andy.

Cari glanced at Andy. He looked worried. Dad never acted this way. Usually the children couldn't wait to search Dad's lunch bucket for leftover goodies. Today, Cari took the bucket to the kitchen and ran back to stand by Dad's chair.

"I'm going to be fine," he said. "I do need to have Mom drive me to the doctor's office in Darrington. My ax slipped, and I cut my foot. We bound it tightly so it would stop bleeding, but I may need stitches."

"Why didn't you go to town in the crew bus?" Cari asked.

"I knew Mom would rather take me." Dad managed to smile. "She'd have to drive me home anyway. Andy, may I lean on your shoulder again?"

About an hour later, the family returned home. The doctor had closed Dad's cut with several neat stitches and wrapped his foot in soft white padding. Now Dad's foot looked like a giant cocoon. The doctor had also given Dad crutches and ordered him to stay out of the woods for a while.

After dinner the telephone rang. "For you, Dad." Andy brought the phone to his father.

Dad was smiling when he hung up the telephone. "Guess what! The Lord has already brought good from this. I was talking with my boss. The company timekeeper just received word his mother is sick. My boss said I could fill in while he's gone. The boss will bring the work to me."

"All right!" Andy shouted. He wrinkled his freckled nose. "Hey, Dad, are there any timekeepers in the forest community?"

Dad laughed. "There sure are. I can show you a timekeeper right here in our yard!"

As soon as Dad was able to walk outside, he led the children to a big stump at the back of their yard. His blue eyes twinkled as he pointed with his crutch. "Here's your timekeeper."

"A *stump?* Are you kidding?" Andy asked.

"No. Look." Dad leaned on a crutch as he bent over to trace the circles on the stump with his finger. "These are called rings. If you count these, you'll discover the age of the tree."

The children started counting. They lost track and had to start over. But Cari said, "This is fun. I'm glad God made forest timekeepers."

"Me too," Andy said. ●

22

Engineers

Andy loved to build things. From the time he was old enough to stack blocks, he built miniature houses, castles, and walls. One day Cari heard an awful sound. *Screech! Screeeeech! Screeeeech! Screeeeech!* She ran outside.

Andy was tearing down his latest project. He called it a caver and a knocker. Every time he pulled a nail from the boards, it made the screeching noise. He was covered with sweat.

"Why are you tearing down your caver and knocker, Andy?" Cari asked.

"I don't want it anymore. It caved in and knocked me on the head!"

"Mom!" Cari hollered.

Mom came running. She looked at the bump on Andy's head and insisted on taking him to the doctor.

"Anyone who gets hit on the head needs to be examined by the doctor," she firmly told them. "Besides, there's a scratch. You may need a tetanus shot."

The doctor examined Andy and said he didn't need a shot. The doctor laughed and patted Andy on the shoulder when Mom told him the story of the caver and knocker.

"Son, you'll probably be an engineer when you grow up," he said.

Cari told Dad what the doctor had said about Andy. She scratched her head and asked, "What does a caver and knocker have to do with running trains?"

Dad laughed. He explained the difference between a railroad engineer who drives trains and an engineer who designs and builds bridges and buildings. "Sunday afternoon I'll show you some forest engineers," he promised.

After eating lunch on Sunday, the Reynolds family set out to explore. Cari and Andy were so eager to see forest engineers they didn't even stop to count the rings on the many stumps left in the fields to see how old the trees were.

Dad led them down a dim, woodsy trail.

Branches crossed the trail over their heads.

"It's like walking in a green tunnel," Mom said.

"Forest engineers are responsible," Dad said.

"I know!" Andy shouted. "The alders and hemlocks. Their branches are all grown together. They make a roof for our green tunnel."

Cari looked up. "Are trees forest engineers?"

"Oh, yes, in more ways than one." Dad wore what Cari and Andy called his mysterious face and kept walking. Soon they came to a chuckling stream that flowed over the trail. A fallen log lying across the stream made a good bridge.

"A bridge!" Cari cried. She jumped up and down. After Dad tested it, they all walked across.

"Show us something else, please, Dad."

"All right. Follow me." Dad led the way to a narrow, deep canyon with fern-covered sides. White water rushed downstream. A gigantic tree had fallen across the canyon.

"That looks so cool!" Andy said. A squirrel and a little brown rabbit hopped across the bridge made by God's forest engineers, the trees. ●

Athletes

23

Athletes

The first snow started falling long before Andy and Cari got off the school bus one afternoon. By the time they changed into old, warm clothing, swirling white flakes had changed the gray day to a beautiful place.

Cari stuck out her tongue so the snowflakes could land and melt on it, but Andy told her to wait a little while before eating the snowflakes.

"The first snow brings down any pollution that's in the air," he explained.

"OK." Cari danced up and down on the whitening ground. "Goody!" she said. "The snow is piling up. It's so beautiful, like a soft white blanket." She lay down in the snow and moved her arms and legs up and down to make a perfect angel outline in the snow.

Before the crew bus stopped in front of the Reynoldses' home, four inches of snow had covered the earth. "If this keeps up, we won't be working for a while," Dad said at the supper table. "It's early for a heavy snowfall, but winter comes when it comes."

"A lot of people will be out of work, won't they?" Andy asked.

"We'll hope it doesn't last too long," Mom said softly.

"Should we ask God to make it quit snowing?" Cari stopped chewing and waited for Dad's answer. She sighed, hoping he wouldn't say yes. She really, really liked playing in the snow.

"Let's just ask God to do what's best for everyone," Dad told her. They did just that when they had family devotions before going to bed.

So much snow fell during the night, neither the crew bus nor the school bus came. The family delighted in their day off. They worked together to shovel trails to the mailbox and the main road. They cleared a space and put out crumbs for the birds and peanuts for the squirrels. Cari kept watch so the scolding blue jays wouldn't steal all the nuts from the squirrels.

Next the Reynolds family built a snow family and tossed soft, spattery handfuls of snow at each other. No snowballs were allowed. Dad said too many people got hurt that way. Then the family went sledding.

When darkness fell, the family stretched out on the rug in front of the hearth, where a cheery fire crackled. Andy talked about all the tumbling he had done in the snow. Then he asked, "Dad, are there athletes in the forest community? We've talked about so many things. It's strange we never thought about forest athletes."

Dad considered for a moment. Then he turned to Mom. "Maybe tonight is a good time to get out the movies we took on our honeymoon. It's been a long time since we looked at them."

Cari blurted out, "What do honeymoon movies have to do with athletes? Did you go to the Olympics for your honeymoon?"

"No, but we saw a lot of forest athletes." Dad grinned.

"They went on a camping trip, 'way up in the mountains," Andy explained.

"Oh," Cari said, but she looked puzzled. She decided she'd just have to wait and see the movies for herself. It had been so long since Dad showed the movies she couldn't remember what was on them.

"God knows His animals must be strong in order to survive," Dad said as he set up the projector and loaded the film. "Watch and see how many athletes you can find."

The first athletes in the film were a pair of bear cubs that walked into a flower-filled meadow. They looked around and began to play. The camera had faithfully captured their wrestling.

"They're athletes!" Cari cried.

"So is he." Andy pointed to a young deer butting its head on a log. Another deer strolled up, and the two deer began a game of hide-and-seek. They sprinted, jumped, and raced. Dad said they were learning survival skills. Someday they would need to leap high and race swiftly to escape danger.

The last athletes in the movies were a pair of cougar cubs. They tumbled and chased each other to develop muscles under their tawny skin. Andy and Cari decided the movie was the next best thing to being there to see more of God's wonderful forest community for themselves! ●

24

Show-offs

Darrington had a mild winter that year. Spring bounded in with equal parts of sunshine and showers. The days grew longer, so the Reynolds family again began exploring the forest.

One day before summer vacation, Andy came home in a terrible mood. He could hardly wait to tell Dad and Mom about one of the kids in his class. "I know we aren't supposed to call people names," Andy muttered. "But Jason acts like a jerk, always trying to impress people."

"Folks—and creatures—who show off usually do try to impress others," Dad agreed.

"Are there show-offs in the forest, too?" Andy asked.

"Yes. I don't have to go to work tomorrow. We'll see what the show-offs will do."

The next morning after eating breakfast and doing their chores, the family headed toward the forest. They needed to wear warm jackets because the morning air was still cool.

"There's your first show-off," Dad said in a low tone when they got halfway across the field behind their home. "Shhh."

Mom and the children froze in place. Before them a male pheasant ruffled his gorgeous feathers and strutted back and forth in front of a less-colorful female pheasant. He advanced and retreated, advanced and retreated.

"He's showing off for his ladylove," Dad said. "Spiders dance for their mates."

Cari couldn't stop looking at the pheasants. In addition to prancing around like a ballet dancer, the male began to make all kinds of noises. He screamed and whistled, cackled and crowed—all to get the female pheasant's attention. She paid him little attention and finally walked away.

"She's ignoring him," Mom whispered.

The male got louder and ruffled his feathers more. Andy couldn't keep silent when the male continued to strut. His shout of laughter alarmed both birds, and they hurried away. "Sorry," Andy whispered as he wiped his eyes. "He was so funny."

"Sometimes show-offs are very funny," Mom agreed.

They didn't find other show-offs that day, but a few weeks later they learned more about them.

On the next Sunday afternoon the Reynolds family packed a lunch and drove a long way up the road that led to Dad's job. After lunch they hiked on trails Dad knew from all his years of living in Darrington. He led the way, carrying a brush hook to clear the little-used path.

When they reached a clearing, Dad held up his hand in the signal that meant they were to stop, look, and listen. Dad took a few steps to the side and made room for the others. "Don't make any noise," he whispered.

Cari covered her mouth to keep from crying out. Four deer stood on the far side of the clearing: a buck, a doe, and two spotted fawns.

"The buck's antlers are still in velvet," Andy whispered in Cari's ear.

"I know," she whispered back.

Dad had taught the children that deer in mild and cold climates lose their antlers each winter and grow new ones in summer.

Fine, short hairs on the soft, new antlers made them look like velvet.

The deer walked closer and closer to where the family stood. The light wind that had been blowing toward the family shifted. It carried human scent to the deer's sensitive noses. The buck snorted and leaped high. He galloped away, and the other deer ran behind him.

That night Dad told the children more about deer. "When the antlers harden, bucks use them to fight for a mate or to keep leadership of the herd. It's their way of proving they are strong and worthy."

Andy thought about this for a while. Then he said, "If Jason felt strong and worthy, maybe he'd stop showing off."

"Perhaps you can think of ways to help him feel that way, Andy," Dad said. "Jesus would be happy if you tried." ●

25

Mourners

I'll take you to the river by a different trail today," Dad said.

Andy walked silently, scuffing his tennis shoes and kicking a smooth stone. He wasn't smiling.

"Dad, when God made the world, why did He make sadness?"

"You're thinking about Terry, aren't you, Andy?"

"Yes." A big lump grew in Andy's throat. "I know we all have to die someday, but Terry was just my age. We were going to do a lot of neat stuff."

Dad sighed. "There aren't any easy answers, Andy. Death entered our world because the people God created chose to disobey Him. We feel sad when we have to say goodbye, but we can be glad because we will see Terry again. He loved the Lord. Someday we will live in a place where no one ever dies."

Tears stung Andy's eyes. "But we have to wait so long."

"Maybe not too long," Mom said. "You know Jesus promised to come back. We don't know when He'll come, but it could be soon."

Andy kicked a rock. "I wish He'd come soon. I miss Terry."

"Did you know that people show their sadness over the loss of friends and loved ones in many ways?" Dad asked. "The Jewish people and others mourn. That means they show their sadness by crying— sometimes very loudly. In Bible times, mourners were paid to cry and shout about their sadness."

Cari had been walking quietly beside Andy. Now she patted his arm. Taking his hand in hers, she said, "Don't feel sad, Andy." She thought for a moment. "Dad, do the forest creatures mourn?"

"Yes," Dad said. "Wolves and other animals that have lost their mates have been known to stand guard by the body. Sometimes they howl or cry."

Andy kicked another rock. Kicking

rocks made him feel a little better. So did what Dad and Mom said about seeing Terry again.

A few days later a strange thing happened. The Reynoldses were on their way to town in the car when Dad braked sharply, swerved, and stopped the car.

"What's wrong?" Cari asked.

"I didn't want to hit the robin sitting in the road. I wonder why it didn't fly away. Let's see what's happening." The family jumped out of the car and ran back to the robin. The little red-breasted bird sat very still, right in the middle of the road. It showed no fear, not even when Dad picked it up and cradled it in his strong hands.

Dad carefully examined the bird. "It's a little male robin. See his bright colors? He couldn't have been hit by a car," he said. "There's no blood on him. His legs and wings are not hurt."

Still the robin sat perfectly still.

"It's like he doesn't even know we're here or where he is," Mom said.

Dad handed Mom the bird. "I wonder . . . His voice trailed off. He looked around the roadside. "Uh-oh. I thought this might be the problem." He called the family to him. The family knelt beside a little robin lying at the side of the road. This little bird's colors were not as bright as the robin Mom was holding.

"His mate," Mom said. "A car must have hit her."

Andy gently touched the living robin's head. So did Cari.

"He must be a mourner," Andy said.

"It looks that way," Dad agreed.

Mom laid the little mourner beside his dead mate. She quietly moved away from the birds.

"Will he be all right?" Cari asked.

"I think he will," Dad told her. "It's just going to take some time for him to mourn his mate."

Andy didn't say anything for a long time. When he did, his blue eyes looked solemn. "I'll be glad when Jesus comes. When we live with Jesus, no person and none of God's other creatures will be sad." ●

26

Night Crew

The Reynolds family sat on the porch, enjoying the gorgeous evening. A yellow cheese moon climbed over the top of a mountain and grinned at them. Millions of stars peeped down to see what was going on. Then Dad asked in a low, mysterious voice, "Who wants to go on a spying adventure?"

"I do," Mom said. She laughed and raised her hand.

"Me too," Cari said.

"Whom are we going to spy on?" Andy wanted to know.

"The night crew," Dad said. He chuckled when he saw the strange expressions on their faces. "Animals that roam at night

Night Crew

are called *nocturnal*," Dad explained. "I just like to call those animals 'the night crew.' Remember the Bible story about how Joshua sent spies into Jericho?"

"Yes," the children answered.

"Those spies probably traveled at night and walked softly. We need to do the same things if we want to see the night crew. Do all of you have on your tennis shoes? Good. Now we each need a flashlight. The moon and stars are making it almost as light as day, but they can't shine through closely woven branches."

Andy and Cari could barely control their excitement. Going into the woods in the daytime and early evening had been wonderful. Getting to spy on the night crew—whoever they were—just had to be better!

They didn't need their flashlights at first. The moon was so bright it made everything look silvery. Just before they got to the edge of the woods, something cried, "Whooo! Whooo! Whooo!" Cari grabbed her mother's hand and cried, "What's that!" She forgot all about being quiet. The spies heard a great rushing sound. Something swooped from a tree branch and sailed away.

"Look!" Dad whispered. He shone his flashlight in the direction of the sound. "There's the first member of the night crew."

"All that noise out of that one old owl?" Andy sputtered.

"Whooo! Whooo! Whooo!" the owl called.

Dad turned off his flashlight. Yet the family of spies could still see the owl as it flew directly between them and the moon.

"I was so scared!" Cari confessed.

"That's nothing to be ashamed of." Dad laughed. "I remember coming home one night after dark. An owl a lot smaller than this one screeched in my ear. It spooked my horse, and I had a terrible time getting him to settle down."

"What else is on the night crew?" Andy wanted to know.

"Follow me. Let's see if we can find some more," Dad said. "Some of these animals actually are around during the daytime, too, but nighttime is a good time to see them."

Dad led his family to a grassy spot overlooking a stream. He warned them again to be quiet and simply wait. The stream bubbled and sparkled in the moonlight, chanting a song on its way to the river that ran to the faraway sea. Cari yawned. Fresh air and the singing stream made her sleepy. But spies must not sleep on the job! She yawned again.

A rustling in the bushes brought her

wide awake. "Don't turn on your flashlights until I tell you to," Dad whispered. Something was chuckling. Then two dark shapes passed close by. "Now!" Dad whispered.

Four streams of light flashed into the dark night, right on two fat porcupines. They turned to look where the family was standing, and their eyes gleamed in the light. The porcupines didn't seem afraid. After a minute one waddled away, and the other followed. They were still chuckling.

Andy remembered not to shout. He formed the "all right!" sign with his fingers and held them up for Dad to see. "What's next?" he whispered.

"Switch off your lights, and wait again," Dad replied.

A little later the spies heard a creaking in the bushes. Black shapes appeared. These members of the night crew turned out to be a mother raccoon and her two small ones walking toward the stream. "They're cute," Cari said. "They should be the spies. They're already wearing little black masks."

On the way home Dad shone his light on a mother opossum. She was carrying her babies in a pouch on her stomach. The mother bared her teeth at them, and the spies quickly walked around her. Dad said possums hunt at night. They often hang upside down from a tree limb by wrapping their tails around a branch. "The expression 'playing possum' comes from the way God made these animals to protect themselves," Dad told the children. "They play dead in times of danger."

"Thank you, Dad, for bringing us to spy on the night crew," the children said. "We'll never forget this adventure." ●

27

Weavers

Andy and Cari loved to talk about their special spying adventure and the night crew they had seen in the forest. "I liked the owl," Andy said. "Whooo! Whooo! Whooo!" He raced around the backyard and flapped his arms like wings.

Cari giggled. "You look funny." She giggled some more. "You look like you are trying to take off."

"I can in my dreams," Andy boasted. "Now I'm a rocket ship." He yelled and leaped into the air. He landed near a huckleberry bush. "Hey, Cari!" Andy shouted. He pointed to a spider's lacy web that was swaying in the wind.

Cari didn't like spiders very well. She

didn't go any closer to the web. She did like looking at the dainty web, though. After dinner she and Andy told Dad and Mom about it.

Dad looked mysterious. "If you wait for just the right time, I'll show you something very, very lovely."

Cari clapped her hands. Andy's eyes shone. "When, Dad?" Cari asked.

"Wait and see" was all the children could get him to say.

A few mornings later when dawn had barely streaked the sky, Dad called the children. "Now is the perfect time to see that very, very lovely surprise I promised you. Slip on shoes and robes and come with me."

Cari and Andy rubbed sleep from their eyes and followed Dad. Mom already stood in the yard.

Cari gasped. Her eyes flew wide open. "There are lace handkerchiefs all over the grass!"

"It certainly looks that way, doesn't it?" Mom agreed. Drops of heavy dew weighed down the webs. Then the first ray of sunlight made the webs sparkle like hundreds of diamonds scattered across the lawn.

Andy grinned. "Cari, those are webs. Spiders wove them in the night. Are they members of the night crew, Dad?"

"They're some of God's weavers," Dad explained. His blue eyes twinkled. "You know how people who fish use nets to catch food? Spiders spin webs to catch insects so they can have food."

"Yuck!" Cari stuck out her tongue and rolled her eyes. "I'm glad God lets spiders make beautiful webs, even if they are to catch insects." ●

28

Landlords

One day when Andy and Cari brought the mail in from the big box that stood by the road, Mom had a letter from an old friend. After reading the letter, Mom wiped a tear from her eye.

"What's wrong, Mom?" Cari climbed into her mother's lap and patted her cheek.

Mom sighed. "It's just that sometimes life is hard. My friend is going to have to move from the little house she's rented for many years."

"Doesn't she like living there now?"

"Oh, yes, but the owner died. His children sold the property. My friend can't pay the amount of money the new owner is charging."

"That's terrible!" Andy said. He put his hands on his hips.

"What's a landlord?" Cari demanded.

"A landlord is someone who owns property and rents it out to others," Mom said. She folded the letter and slipped it back into the envelope. "Fortunately, my friend has a son who wants her to come live with him."

"Why doesn't God make landlords be nice?" Cari asked.

"God allows us to choose the way we act. Not all landlords are Christians," Mom replied.

That night the family talked about landlords. Andy asked his dad, "Are there landlords in the forest?"

"Yes, there are, Andy. We'll see if we can find some forest landlords after supper."

The family whisked through the dishes. They were glad for the long summer evenings that once again allowed them to explore.

"How will I know a landlord if I see one?" Cari asked. She looked up at Dad.

"Just remember that a landlord owns space that's occupied—that means filled—by someone or something else."

Cari thought about what Dad said. She looked and looked, but she didn't find anything that could be called a landlord. Just then a small rabbit hopped out of a hollow log. Cari forgot all about being quiet in the forest. "Mom, Dad, Andy!" she hollered. "Is the log a landlord?"

"Good job, Cari," Daddy said. "See if you can find others."

Andy spotted the next landlord when he saw insects busily crawling in and out of an old stump. Blackberry vines grew from its sides. "That old stump is a landlord," he said.

"Ssh," Cari said. She stopped to listen to the sound that came from above her.

Cheep! Cheep! Cheep!

Cari tilted her head back to look up into the leafy green branches of a maple tree. Where two branches crossed, a mother bird had carefully built her nest. Small, naked-looking birds lay in the nest cheeping for something to eat.

Cari whispered, "The tree is also a landlord. Its branches even help keep the birds' nest safe."

Cari stood very still. The mother bird flew into the nest. A long worm dangled from her mouth. Excited cries from the nest told the explorers that the baby birds were hungry for their supper.

"Time to go," Dad announced. "How do you like God's landlords?" he asked.

"I love them!" Cari answered. Andy nodded his head yes.

Mom added, "So do I. Now I just wonder what you're going to show us next," she told her husband.

Dad just smiled. Cari's and Andy's eyes sparkled with mischief. They said together, "You have to wait and see!" ●

Housekeepers

29

Housekeepers

I get tired of doing housework," Andy said one morning. He jabbed the dust mop into a corner of the kitchen. "If we lived in the forest, we'd never, ever have to do housework again."

"Really, Andy?" Dad asked. A smile tugged at the corners of his mouth. His eyes twinkled as if he had a surprise.

"I don't *think* there is any housework to do in the forest." Andy scratched his head. "I won't say for sure, though. Sometimes Dad proves me wrong."

"Are there really housekeepers in the forest?" Cari asked.

"Yes. Really and truly," Dad answered. "We'll see some of them. We won't see all of the housekeepers, but we'll find places where they have cleaned."

When they returned from their nature walk, Andy began scribbling notes so he wouldn't forget the names of the housekeepers they had seen. He would list them on his second poster. He talked aloud while he wrote. "Rivers, streams, and even floods clean the forest floor. Forest fires burn up dead trees and fallen branches. Birds and squirrels throw out old nest material and replace it with new."

"The garbage collectors do their part, too," Cari reminded Andy.

"There are two important things to list," Dad said when Andy showed him his list. "Can you guess what they are?" He gave them a clue. "They work together, cleaning and sweeping and dusting." Dad chuckled.

Finally Andy cried, "I know! Wind and rain. They take the pollution from the air. They work together to remove leaves and dust from the trees."

"How could God make so many wonderful things?" Cari asked for the gazillionth time.

"Because He's God," Andy reminded her. He was glad he was learning enough to help answer some of his little sister's questions. ●

Entertainers

"Mom, why don't we watch TV more often?" Andy asked on one rainy afternoon.

Mom looked up from mending a pair of Andy's jeans. "A lot of television programs aren't good to watch," she said.

"Sure, Mom, they're not good for kids to watch." Andy grinned. "But you and Dad are grown-ups, and you still don't watch much television."

"If we invited Jesus to come visit us, what's the first thing we'd do?" Mom asked quietly.

"Clean house!" Cari said.

"That's right." Mom smiled at her bright-eyed daughter. "We've all asked

Jesus to live in our hearts and minds, so they must be kept clean, too."

Andy thought of some of the programs and videos he'd watched in his friends' homes. "It's just entertainment, Mom," he protested.

Dad had been standing in the doorway while Mom was talking. "God's entertainers don't laugh at sin or make fun of people," he explained. "We do watch a few good programs, such as nature specials," he added. "In fact, television and movie producers can find some real entertainers in the forest."

"Really, Dad?" Cari ran to where Dad stood.

Dad smiled and tousled Cari's hair. "Really. When the rain stops, we'll go find some."

A few hours later the hot sun came out to dry the wet grass. As the family walked beneath the trees, Cari looked at two beautiful orange-and-black butterflies fluttering just a few inches in front of her face. The butterflies swooped, touched each other, then did a fantastic dance in the air.

"They're monarchs!" Andy proudly identified the insects.

"They're also entertainers," Dad said. "They are more graceful than any dancer or ice skater on TV. God gifted them with natural ability, but people have to practice hard to learn to leap and swoop and bend." He laughed.

The butterflies flew away, and the family walked farther into the woods and came to a stream.

Splash!

Cari jumped in surprise. Dad gently parted the brush at the side of the stream. He held his fingers to his lips to signal silence. He motioned for the family to slip through the brush and sit on the rocks by the side of the stream.

"O-o-oh!" Cari sucked her breath in. Across the stream, two large dark-brown animals and two smaller ones dove into the water. They swam and tumbled. They twisted and turned in the water.

"Otters," Dad whispered.

One of the smaller otters dove under the water but didn't swim back to the top quickly. Cari gripped Dad's arm.

"Don't worry," Dad said and patted Cari's arm. "Otters can stay underwater for three to four minutes." Just then the otter's slightly flattened head surfaced. Soon Cari could see the animal's thick neck and pointed tail.

"Wow!" Andy whispered. "Look at that!"

He nodded toward the opposite side of the stream. An otter waddled out of the water and climbed the bank. *Whoosh! Splash!* The otter slid down the side of the bank and into the water. The other otters followed. *Whoosh! Splash! Whoosh! Splash! Whoosh! Splash!*

Cari couldn't hold back her giggles. At the sound, all four otters slid into the water and disappeared. "They'll climb out under a ledge where they live," Dad explained.

All the way home the children talked about God's entertainers. Dad was right. They were funnier and more interesting to watch than any show on television. ●

31

Runaways

The next evening Dad led the family to the stream where they had seen the playful otters. But that night many fish swam upstream, their silver scales flashing in the evening light.

"Salmon are runaways," Dad said. "These salmon were born in freshwater. They swam to the ocean and spent most of their lives in saltwater. Scientists have tagged fish and discovered they go home to spawn—that means they lay their eggs. They leap waterfalls and struggle hard to swim back to the stream where they were born. Some fish swim 2,000 miles to get back home."

Andy and Cari watched the fish that

were fighting their way upstream. They saw salmon leap high into the air to get over small waterfalls. "How do they know their own streams, Dad?" Andy asked.

"Scientists believe each home stream has a certain odor and that the salmon remember it. In any case, God created salmon so perfectly they know their own homes."

"Just as we know our real home is in heaven with Jesus," Mom said.

Andy stared at the leaping fish. Even the runaway son in the Bible hadn't run that far from home. ●

32

Optimists

Although the Reynolds family knew they would take many more trips to the forest and see wonderful things, Dad said he had shown them almost everything in the forest community they could see near Darrington.

"I'm going to take the time now to finish my second poster," Andy said. His completed poster looked like this.

THE FOREST COMMUNITY, NO. 2

Athletes	Choir
bears	grouse
deer	pheasants
cougars	frogs

Collectors

crows
packrats

insects
birds

Engineers

trees
branches
logs

Entertainers

butterflies
otters

Firefighters

rain
ants

Fishers

ducks
raccoons
bears
otters
martens

Guides

Jesus
geese
wild horses
wolves
bees

Housekeepers

rivers
streams
forest fires
birds
squirrels
wind
rain

Landlords

stumps
trees
hollow logs

Night Crew

owls
porcupines
raccoons
opossums

Mourners
birds
wolves

Pilots
eagles
flying insects

Police
gophers
skunks
ants
wasps
fireflies
birds
termites

Runaways
salmon

Show-offs
pheasants
deer

Timekeepers
trees
stumps

Travelers
hermit crabs
geese
swallows

Weather Forecasters
birds
rabbits
squirrels
bears

Weavers
spiders

The two posters hung side by side in the Reynoldses' family room. Just about every day Andy stopped to look at his work. Sometimes he read every word on the posters. Cari liked to run her fingers over the words. She could read all of them now.

One day at the dinner table Dad said, "I have a riddle for you."

"Goody!" Cari clapped her hands, and Andy leaned forward in his chair. Dad's riddles were always fun.

Dad began the riddle. "Someone in this family is like many things in the forest community. I'll give you some hints. All the forest creatures carry out the purposes for which they are created. They are what we call *optimists*. That means, no matter how tough things are, they refuse to stay sad. After a storm wet birds shake their feathers and sing. Rain beats down the flowers, but the flowers lift their heads toward their Creator and bloom again."

Dad paused so the children could think about the clues he had just given. Then he continued. "The person I'm thinking of is optimistic, just like the forest creatures and flowers. She has gone through sickness and pain but always had a smile and never complained."

"Mom!" Andy shouted.

"Mom!" Cari echoed.

Mom smiled and said, "God helped me. I remembered the saying, 'If you walk with your face toward the sun, the shadows will always be behind you.' Andy, Cari, there's an even more important secret than those we talked about in the forest. Remember how Dad went ahead and cleared a path for us so we wouldn't get lost? Our heavenly Father sent Jesus to make a path. He's there to help us walk over rough ground, just as Dad helped us get over fallen logs on the trail."

That night the family had evening devotions on the wide back porch. Andy looked toward the woods where they had spent so many happy hours. A silver moon smiled from the top of a nearby mountain. They heard the cottonwood leaves rustling in the gentle breeze.

Che-runk!

Cari and Andy laughed. "That frog is singing again tonight!" Andy said.

"Now I know that sound is a singing frog and not some other animal," Cari said, and she smiled up at Mom.

"Jesus has planted many things in the forests for us to enjoy. Discovering His secrets helps keep us happy while we are waiting for Him to come and take us home. Let's tell Him." Dad bowed his head. So did the others. One by one Dad, Mom, Cari, and Andy thanked God for His wonderful secrets of the forest. ●

The Professor Appleby and Maggie B Series

Charles Mills and Ruth Redding Brand team up to bring you some of the best Bible stories you've ever heard. Wrapped in a plot you're going to love!

An eccentric old professor receives mysterious boxes from his world-traveling sister Maggie B. Boxes bursting with intriguing artifacts and life-changing stories of people who dared to stand for God.

Join Professor Appleby and his young friends to listen to Maggie B's stories bring the Bible to life!

1. Mysterious Stories From the Bible
Abraham and Sarah, Lot, Joseph, Rahab, Joshua, Hannah and Samuel, and Jesus as a child.

2. Amazing Stories From the Bible
Moses and the Exodus, Samson, Esther, and Jesus' miracles.

3. Love Stories From the Bible
Adam and Eve, Abraham and Sarah, Isaac and Rebekah, Jacob and Rachel, Ruth and Boaz, David and Abigail, and Jesus' first miracle.

4. Adventure Stories From the Bible
Samuel, Saul, David, Solomon, and Hezekiah.

5. Miracle Stories From the Bible
Moses, Elijah, Elisha, Dinah, Joash, and Jesus' miracles.

Each paperback features challenging activities and is US$8.99, Cdn$12.99. Look for more books in the series coming soon.